THE EDGE OF BLISS

CHERIL N. CLARKE

DodiPress

TRIGGER WARNING

This book contains mature sexual themes and situations. It is intended for adults. It also contains depictions of abduction, restraint, threats of violence, and other potentially disturbing situations. Reader discretion is advised.

LEENA'S THOUGHTS...

All I want
>*Is to stand barefoot in the rain*
>*To sing, to dance*
>*To strip from my clothing*

I want to lose it all. Everything.
>*Bra*
>*Panties*
>*Let them tumble to the ground*

I want to walk in the sparkling drops from God unjudged by the thoughts of man
>*To unearth pleasures that have become entombed in decades of proper living*
>*I want to be free*
>*I want to be me*
>*I just want to be*
>*Liberated*

1

I have this desire inside of me, deep and insatiable. I can feel it pulsing like an unstoppable flood. It's anchored in my womb, primal and intrinsically tied to my being ... suppressed for far too long. From the outside looking in, my life is picturesque – perfect even, to some, but there's an essential part of me clamoring for freedom. Dying for attention. Grasping for repeated orgasms of cataclysmic proportion. In the midnight of my soul is a labyrinth of licentious thoughts that leads to one man. His name is Michael. It's been almost three years since I've seen him, but later tonight we're finally going to be alone again. God, how I've been waiting for this!

Michael and I met at a time when my life was much simpler. When I was younger, before scaling the corporate ladder at heel-breaking pace. Before the estate and vacation home, before I'd settled down into restrained comfort and unwitting, self-imprisoning portrayals of perfection. Michael was a fling who was supposed to disappear into the forgotten. But he never did. We never had a traditional relationship and seemingly flowed into each other's lives only during bad times. It was probably better that way. Michael and I are volcanic.

"I don't know what it is about you that's so intoxicating," he always says, "I can never get enough." He freely admits that no matter what we start chatting about inevitably ends up with us being torturously aroused. "You just have this effect on me. Talking to you sends embers of desire rippling under my skin."

"Likewise." I blush.

"I couldn't stop them if I wanted to," he adds incredulously.

"Neither can I," I typically respond. The feeling was mutual.

There's always a dormant lust for Michael in me. Memories of our moments together bring flurries to my stomach. Sighs of pleasure run through me as I close my eyes and lose myself in thoughts of him. He is a spectacular lover, and I craved time alone with him for longer than I wanted to admit.

Our attraction was effortless – the kind of magnetism that's dangerous if not carefully managed. Addictive. So yes, perhaps it was best that the universe only allowed us to collide every so often. But tonight was the night. I'd waited long enough. I *needed* this man inside me.

"Jameson?" I called out to my protection dog to shower him with love before my chauffer arrived to shuttle me to the airport. "Come here, big boy!" I was such a sucker for this Rottweiler. He cost an average American's annual salary but was worth every penny. I felt safe around him than the bodyguard my husband hired for me after our second home was burglarized while I was there alone. "Are you gonna miss me, Jameson? You better!" I touched my nose to his and scratched his ears.

Yes, I'm married, but it's not what you think. My husband is sort of a cuckold. He knows about my feelings of sexual deprivation and has obliged in my quest to quench my body's thirst elsewhere. Although quite honestly, I've never done anything like this before. I've never flown to an exotic island to meet another man with whom I'd had virtual foreplay of the imagination for the greater part of a year – that's how long it had been since Michael and I started chatting again.

I've only been with one other person since getting married but I wasn't as mentally prepared for the act as I'd thought ... so I never called him again. It's different now. Michael is the exception, and my husband is a strange kind of amazing for allowing this escapade.

I really don't like the term cuckold, however, because it has a negative connotation. I love my husband dearly. He has taken my well of carnal urges and encouraged the help of other men to fulfill my needs whether he's involved or not. It's not that he's inadequate in bed – he's actually amazing. He's just not enough. I need it a lot. My body is an ocean of sexual energy potent beyond measure. Besides, he revels in hearing about me being with another man and fantasizes about it openly with me. It's different and taboo for most couples, but I've grown used to it. The fact that my husband's desires allows me to be with Michael and not feel guilty is sublime.

There was just one problem: Michael didn't know I was married and I still wasn't sure I should tell him. I didn't want to scare him off.

ETA: 15 minutes. My cell phone vibrated with a text message from my driver.

I couldn't believe the day was finally here. My stomach was a knot of zeal. In just five hours I'd touch down in Turks and Caicos and be ferried to an opulent villa away from the all-inclusive resorts that most people flock to.

Thanks, Steve, I'll be ready. I exhaled and sent Michael a message that I was heading to the airport.

Perfect, I'm already in flight!;) He responded within minutes.

Jesus, this man ... I felt a throb in the crease of my thighs and a tremble in my chest.

"Mrs. West, good morning." Steve arrived faster than I realized. He greeted me with a smile when I open the door.

"Good morning." I returned the grin. We exchanged pleasantries as he took my bags to the to my car. I said goodbye to Jameson before sliding into the backseat of my Maserati. Steve's vehicle was parked in my guest spot until he returned.

∾

IT WAS A GORGEOUS SPRING DAY, and the 40-minute ride to the Newark airport was uneventful. I held back on texting Michael again, wanting to give myself time to imagine how the next three days were going to go. We'd discussed so many scenarios that it was impossible to know how many we'd fulfill, or which ones. I did take a few items to ensure I bring to life an experience Michael has made clear he wanted to explore, but only with me. I quivered at the idea and bit my lip to soak in the sultry thoughts. I adjusted my shades self-consciously, hoping Steve wasn't paying attention to me.

"Well, here we are, Mrs. West." Steve jolted me out of my thoughts as he pulled into the drop-off area for departing international flights. "United Airlines, right?"

"That's it." Girlish excitement washed over me as I stepped out of my car and waited for Steve to retrieve my bags. It was a Tuesday and relatively calm as far as other passengers went.

"Have a safe flight. I'll be checking your arrival status to be here when you get back in town."

"Thanks so much!"

"My pleasure," he nodded affirmatively before sliding back in the driver's seat.

Steve was a semi-retired, older gentleman who had a jolly personality and air of polish. He'd been driving me off and on for the last couple of years and was genuinely a pleasure to be around. His easygoing nature came in handy when I was stressed out and feeling overwhelmed from work. On days like today, his service allowed me to sink deeply into my thoughts without having to worry about the logistics of travel – and I'm grateful. Life was beautiful.

IT TOOK ALMOST no time to get to the United Club with my priority check-in and TSA pre-check security status. The Club wasn't the best airport lounge I'd killed time in and felt a bit crowded, but it beat sitting at the gate overrun with a mass of travelers scouting power outlets and filthy seats. It was a decent consolation for the fact that I couldn't fly privately for this tryst.

The moment I settled down with a drink and bite to eat, however, I got a message from the airline. My flight had been delayed thirty minutes due to a mechanical issue with the aircraft. *Great. Just great.*

I can't wait to hear about your trip when you get back. A message from my husband cascaded in right after the airline's. *I miss you already but am so thrilled about this!* He confessed.

I was still bewildered by this sometimes. My husband, Phillip, is unlike any other man I've ever known. Green-eyed and stocky with ginger-colored skin, he was a rare breed. His family was from the Bahamas, but he'd been living in the States for more than twenty years. We met on a wine valley tour and developed an unlikely attraction that was strong enough to lead us to the altar. He's quirky – too worldly to describe in everyday terms, but I adore him.

I miss you too; I texted him back. *And the thought of you anticipating this is turning me on more than I imagined.* I told the truth. It's fascinating how something you thought you'd never understand can become an act that stimulates you. When Phillip first told me that he would be fine if I slept with another man I thought he was insane – or gay, and just looking for a cover for *him* to be with other men. But neither was true. He's genuinely turned on by it, and his unique fetish awakened a part of me that I never knew existed a – part that could not only accept and be okay with this but indulge and build upon it. Breaking the conventional rules of marriage can create indescribable pockets of intimacy and complexity between people.

Maybe next time I'll join, he added with a devilish smiley.

My body tensed at the thought of both men craving me. Perhaps one day I could be with them at the same time. The idea intrigued me, but I quickly brushed it off. Right then I wanted Michael to have me all to himself and vice versa.

Tell me more... Phillip pressed me, tugging my attention back to him. He loved sexting.

I told him how eager I was to feel Michael inside of me and how I longed to trace the contours and muscular details of his skin – Michael's, not my husband's – with my tongue and fingertips. I painted a picture of Michael hoisting me on his shoulders and devouring me against an ivory wall, of him tearing off the exquisite lingerie that Phillip bought me and burrowing his face into the most sensitive crevices of my body. Phillip was excited. I could feel it through his messages. I felt passion build between my legs. I needed to get on that plane.

"What do you mean the flight is delayed again?" I heard a neighboring passenger angrily yelling into his phone.

I'd gotten so caught up with Phillip I didn't realize there was another postponement. *Damn it!* I was starting to get annoyed now. The lounge had gotten even more crowded and was probably just barely better than the main waiting area. Irate travelers were the last thing I wanted to be surrounded by on this day. I was ready to get going, to be on my way to meet Michael.

"Are there any other flights to Providenciales?" I get up to ask an airline employee. "To Turks and Caicos," I clarify. "I'll pay the change fee."

"I'm sorry, ma'am, but all other flights are completely booked."

"Do you know how much longer it'll be?"

"We're hoping to have the issue resolved within the next hour," she said apologetically. "Hopefully sooner."

"All right, fine." I knew there was no point in getting upset with her. After all, if something was wrong with the aircraft that's the last place I want to be. But I did need to get to my beau and not squander any more time than I'd already been forced to.

I decided to check other airlines, but none had any flights going out any sooner. Not even to Grand Turk, the next closest airport. Frustration gnawed at me, but I fought it. It would be another hour and three more glasses of wine before I finally boarded the plane. Getting a step closer to taking the flight perked me up a bit. I sent Michael another message letting him know that I was finally on my way.

I will be waiting for you. He responded. *I'm so excited!* He added with a smiley face and handsome selfie attached.

With skin the color of coconut palm tree bark, Michael's face was an island of features. He had hazel eyes and a chiseled jawline adorned with a full beard and mustache. It was a type of manliness unlike what I was used to, and I loved it. Well dressed and well groomed, Michael had an air of urban sophistication about him. I couldn't wait to run my fingers over his head.

You look delicious, I gushed. I could imagine him staring at me with those sexy eyes. He had a way of squinting that made me feel as though he were reeling me into his gaze by the sheer strength and depth of it. Michael's gaze was piercing. I told him how I ached to feel his strong hands all over my body, ready to bend to the will of his might.

Before I could say much more, however, I was reminded by a flight attendant that it was time to turn off my phone for take-off. *Thank God!* I sent one last message to let him know I was finally on the way. I felt a rush as the plane slowly began taxiing away from the airport. The red flash of the brake lights popped onto the tarmac in a staccato rhythm that mirrored the punches of anxiety that cut through my exhilaration about this trip. I couldn't have predicted the mix of feelings that swirled inside of me at that moment.

As the aircraft slowly made its way down the runway, I began scrolling through my phone and looking at a catalog of my favorite photos of Phillip. From silly selfies that made me beam with pride to endearing photos of us that made me question the reality of my current choice. What if this was a big mistake? Would Phillip really be okay? What about me? I thought about Michael. I was really looking forward to seeing him but wondered if I were playing with a fire I couldn't extinguish. I was excited but felt still guilty; nervous yet eager. My emotions ricocheted before slinking down into a neutral place of acceptance of whatever the outcome and a promise to take care of my marriage at all costs. *Don't overthink it* I told myself, and pivoted to more pleasure-filled fantasies about my impending rendezvous.

2

ours later I awakened to endless views of shimmering turquoise waters. Between the wine, the meals, and the comfort of my first-class pod, I'd drifted off to sleep. It was only my eager dreams of being tangled with Michael that roused me in time to catch the gorgeous areal views. I woke up wet with anticipation and was ever grateful for the privacy of my space against the window so I could compose myself.

I sent a message letting Michael know that I'd be landing shortly and he told me that he already knew. He'd been tracking my flight so that he'd be there the moment I stepped off the plane. Excitement swept the entirety of my being as the jet get glided over Caribbean waters. *I hope I'm all that he remembers me to be.* I chuckled at the thought. *Of course I am, I'm better than I used to be!* I pumped myself up and smiled at my inner back and forth. This meeting was making me feel like a twenty-year-old again.

The swirling gemstone waters in my view reflected my fluttering feelings, and the arch of the deep blue sea around the turquois shore reminded me of all the things Michael wanted to venture into. We had already experienced bliss in traditional sexual adventures, but were yearning to wade into the depths of our desires just to see how much we could endure. How deep could we go? How much more could we discover about each other in just a few days? And just how much sexual power will I unleash on him? Questions pounded against each other in my mind.

"Ladies and gentlemen, as we start our descent, please make sure your seat backs and tray tables are in their full upright position," a flight attendant announced. "Make sure your seat belt is securely fastened and all carry-on luggage is stowed underneath the seat in front of you or in the overhead bins. Thank you."

It was finally time! The next 20 minutes were a blur and just as soon as I hoped, I was greeted by this gorgeous mass of a man, Michael. I saw exhilaration in his eyes the moment I appeared in his field of view. My heart skipped a beat. *Keep it together,* I reminded myself.

"Leela." He broke into a smile as my name fell from his lips. He outstretched his confident arms and pulled me into an engulfing embrace.

"Michael..." I got on toes to wrap my arms around his neck and let myself melt in his warm embrace. He was wearing *Acqua Di Gio* by Armani, an arousing cologne I never got tired of. I wondered earlier if he recalled how I fawned over the scent on him years ago. He was always good at remembering details.

For as long as I waited for this moment, I found myself at a loss for words. I just wanted to look at him. To feel him and become entangled with him. Neither of us said much for the first few moments, preferring to soak in the long-awaited unfolding of our reunion. I eventually took a step back and admired him once more. He was dressed simply, but gave off extraordinary confidence; a fitted V-neck t-shirt that showed off his shoulders and arms gave a teasing reveal of his tattooed chest. An onyx necklace with a tribal tiger tooth pendant glimmered against his white top.

"You look gorgeous," he complimented before my eyes could travel below his waist. "Stunning, as usual," he added.

"Thank you, so do you." I was ready to leave without my luggage, but I kept my enthusiasm at bay.

"I love your hair like this!" He smiled broadly and looked me over from head to toe.

I'd decided to wear my hair in a natural halo of kinky curls instead of straightened. My tresses reached the middle of my back when flat ironed, but lately I'd been enjoying my locks in their normal state. "Thank you," I blushed.

"Let's grab your bags," he insisted and took my hand.

It didn't take long to retrieve my things from the luggage carousel and before I knew it, we were on our way to our villa. The ten-minute ride to Taylor Bay felt like two and the sun was gracefully bowing out for the night by the time we arrived. A blaze of orange glory filled the sky and warm night air flowed welcomingly through the car. It had been a long day and I was genuinely exhausted. I couldn't wait to settle in for the evening.

"I figured you'd be hungry so I've ordered already ordered dinner," Michael said with a grin as we pulled into the driveway of our rental.

"Thank you. I am." I could feel him glancing at me every so often. He grabbed my bags and led the way. I followed closely but with enough distance to admire his back and ass. This man was beautiful.

The entrance was unassuming but the villa itself is stunning. It was at least 4,000 square feet with an infinity pool overlooking the ocean and an outdoor shower, a massive kitchen with two stoves, multiple balconies, an umbrella deck and more rooms than we needed but enough that we could to try to christen each more than once. The master suite had double doors that opened to startling views of nature's perfection. Flanked by palm trees and masterfully designed, the sights from inside property had already relaxed me.

"So, what do you think?" Michael slid his hands around my waist, and we shared a moment looking out to the ocean.

"It's amazing. I love it!" I smiled widely and turned to face him.

"I can't believe I finally have you to myself again," he exclaimed. "It's been so many years."

"But I still remember your touch like it was yesterday."

He blushed.

"I think about you often," I added. "Even when we had stopped speaking for a while, you were never far from my thoughts."

"The same for me. We've had too many amazing times for you to ever be buried too deeply in my memory." He pulled me close and wrapped his arms around me so that we both faced the ocean. The muscles in his chest pressed against my back.

I inched my hips and ass back just enough so that I could feel his muscles located elsewhere. He gently bit my neck with a subtle hunger for me. I could feel his appetite growing with each proceeding kiss.

Michael and I enjoyed the evening outside over dinner and a bottle of white wine. We caught up on things that had happened over the years and relived memories of some of our most tantalizing times —the sizzle of making love in front of a hotel window in a room filled with a hundred tea candles, or the time I slid my hand in his pants and stroked him near the point of explosion while on an evening horse and carriage ride, and vivid flashbacks of meeting in the United Kingdom and having public sex at sunset at Tennyson Down, a breathtaking cliff on the edge of the ocean. I'll never forget that one.

I became enraptured in the journey down memory lane and soon found myself squirming with anticipation of feeling him inside me again. I leaned in to kiss him and felt a flush between my legs. My nipples hardened and my breasts felt full. They became needy, clamoring for his attention. I ran my hands up his vascular arms and cupped his neck while sinking deeper in osculation, entwining my tongue with his. Michael's beard grazed my face when planted his lips on other parts of me. He pecked my cheeks, my forehead and bit my earlobes. Michael breathed heavily, yearningly, as he journeyed the details of my face and neck with adoration.

"Mmm." I couldn't hold back my moans. "Michael..."

"Yes?" He asked breathlessly. He craved me just as badly as I wanted him, but was measured in his approach.

I climbed on top of him, rocking and swaying, already inebriated with the energy between us – never mind the wine. He grabbed me at my hips and slid a hand under my shirt, pushing my panties aside. I buckled at the feel of his fingertips wandering up my thighs to find a warm home in between them. I began to gyrate without thought. I buried my lips in the crux of his neck, biting and sucking and kissing as much of his skin as I could reach.

"Oh, shit. Leela..." He thrust upward into me.

I held onto him tighter, a slight tremble traveling from my wrists up my forearms.

Michael unfastened my bra with ease. His touch felt like cashmere caressing my bare skin. Covered by a dark sky specked with thousand glittering stars, I began unbuttoning my blouse so he could completely disrobe me. The night air got hot, and we panted with desire for each other. But at some point, something felt off. I couldn't help but notice Michael's energy changed. He seemed distracted as we continued to make out. Our connection was broken.

"Is everything okay?" I leaned back to give him space.

He exhaled but didn't say anything.

"What's wrong?" I knew for sure something is bothering him now and eased off him.

"It's just..." he began, but struggled to continue.

"Just what?" I felt nervous. *Did I do something*?

He hesitated again but finally blurted it out. "The ring." He looked down. "You're wearing a wedding ring."

Shit! I had totally forgotten I about it; and worse, that Michael knew nothing about my marriage. "Oh. That." I mumbled. *Fuck!* The timing of this conversation couldn't have been worse.

"I don't know if I can do this if..." he began, but doesn't even need to finish. This had to be terrible for him to think about.

Goddamn it. Michael had recently divorced his wife of eighteen years after she cheated on him for the second time. It hadn't been long enough for the pain of repeated betrayal to subside. The thought of me possibly doing the same to my husband rubbed him the wrong way, or at least that's how I rationalized his shock. My heartbeat thudded in my chest. The shivers of passion I had just been feeling quickly disintegrated into shards of nervousness. I had messed up.

"It's not what you think," I rushed to explain.

"So you're not married?" He eyed me suspiciously.

"I am, but I'm not cheating on him."

Michael's face crumpled in perplexity.

"He knows that I'm with you," I confessed, but quickly realized that made the situation even more awkward. "I mean, he's not against me being with other men." I tried to clean it up.

"What?" Michael scooted away, his face a picture of bewilderment.

I took a moment to gather my thoughts and explain my marital arrangement as candidly as possible. "I know it's different," I began, "but I promise you I'm telling the truth," I pleaded with him.

He looked a sour mix of hurt and betrayed as I shared my situation. "So, you're not single?" Michael processed the information again.

"No," I said quietly. I felt like shit.

He exhaled harshly.

I tried my best to assure him that my intentions were pure. The last thing I wanted was to remind him of the woman who shattered his heart. God, how stupid of me to forget about my ring! He wasn't the kind of guy who would carelessly ignore that kind of symbol.

"I'm sorry I didn't tell you sooner," I offered. "I just didn't know how. It's not your traditional marriage setup and ... and I guess I was just afraid of how you might respond."

Michael clasped his hands together. "I wish you had given me a choice – asked if I would be okay with this."

"I'm so sorry."

Michael sat quietly. Unreadable.

I'd caught him off guard and reality had smeared the mood we were sharing just moments ago. "Please," I appealed. "I really didn't mean to put you in such an awkward position. I apologize. I was wrong for not telling you up front. I'm sorry!" Regrets hurled themselves from me in rueful form.

He sighed.

I reached for him and cautiously touched his hand. "Do you

believe me?" I really wanted this man and didn't want to fly home in embarrassment. "I promise you I'm telling the truth."

"I do, actually," he spoke quietly. "I trust you not to lie to me." His words were the comfort I'd been hoping for. "It's just a lot to process, you know? I thought I was your only one." Michael ran his hands over his head and let out a nervous chuckle. "He's a cuck. Wow."

I hated hearing the term, but not more than I wanted to repair this moment. "He's a wonderful man who is okay with me retaining my sexual independence."

Michael raised both hands slightly as if to gesture an apology for uttering the word. "I get it."

"So ... are you okay with this?" I looked him directly in his eyes. "Do you still want me?"

He curled his lips inward and rubbed his left hand over his face. His right leg shook nervously; just a little, but enough for me to notice. He nodded affirmatively before the words fell from his mouth. "Yeah, I think so." A naughty smile spread across his face.

I couldn't tell if his shock had morphed into intrigue or what exactly he was feeling, but I'd gotten my answer. It was a go. *Selfish*, I thought – a part of me chastised my relief at his decision. I downed the last of the wine that was in my glass and flung the moral version of me out my mind. My heartbeat began to moderate to a normal pace after having raced off with the stress of the moment. I suppressed a bashful smile.

"It's cool," he assured me and pulled me back toward him. "It's actually kind of thrilling – the thought of sleeping with another man's wife with his permission." Michael ripped off my blouse with new vigor. He spread his legs to give his manhood room to expand. He looked at me with tiger-like intensity. "Fucking you tonight is going to be really special." I could feel him growing harder against me.

"I want you so badly," I managed to say in between my weighted breaths.

I pulled Michael's face into my chest, unable to wait for his lips to touch my skin again. The slick warmth of his tongue circling the outline of my breasts made my body lurch with anticipation. I whispered how much I loved and missed his touch and became enraptured with the long trails of licks, kisses and nips he placed all over my upper body. Michael gave attention to everything from my forehead to my collar bones, down to the curves of my sides and flexes of my hips.

"I've been thinking about this moment for so long," I confessed as we explored each other fervently.

Michael didn't respond verbally but the power of his groans told me he felt the same way. He picked me up and carried me into the villa. It took no time for him to hoist me against a wall; my skirt bunched around my waist and my legs wrapped around his waist, arms draped over his shoulders. He kissed me voraciously as I clung to him with all my strength.

"Let's go in the shower." Michael's lips were so close to my ear he ended his question with a nibble on my lobe.

I will go anywhere with you right now, I thought, but just mumbled, "Mm-hm."

He winked and let me get my feet on the ground before leading me to the master suite. By the time we were under the showerhead my wetness had slid onto my thighs. Michael lit up at the sticky feel of me on his finger as he pushed one inside of me. He flashed a ravenous smile and grew visibly more erect. He glided another finger inside me and began to slowly caressing my clitoris and stroked my inner walls with a beckoning motion while lowering to his knees. I braced myself against for the sensation of Michael enjoying me. He sucked me hungrily.

Michael relished pleasing me and became more vocal with each plunge of his fingers and stroke of his tongue. His moans created a vibration around my slit that made me shiver. He pulled his fingers out only to put one of my legs on his shoulder and devour me from another angle. My other leg began to tremble. The bathroom filled with steam and I became woozy from the tenacity of his tongue and kisses. It wasn't long before we writhed in the carnal tempo of our lust-filled desires. Michael grabbed my ass and spread me open further, letting his tongue dip well below where he'd started.

"Oh my God!" I gasped. The feeling was exhilarating. I began thrusting my hips into his face as he caressed my lower back. Michael buried his tongue deeper into the fount of my nectar. When it became too intense, I pushed his head away so that I could return the elation.

"Come here," I called him off his knees and began lowering to mine before he was fully standing.

Michael was ripe. He looked strong and delicious. I was eager to let my tongue stroke and flow and flick over the tip of his arousal. I wanted to suck the length of him while massaging his sack with one hand and grabbing his ass with the other. The moment I was in position I went to work. Michael bellowed on contact. I was so eager to taste him, I took as much of him as I could handle right away, guiding him to pump me full. He rocked and swayed as I showered his stiff lingam with attention my mouth and hands. Michael held me at my shoulders and fed me his thick inches. The water streamed down on us and before we knew it our exhilaration was reaching a frantic pace. I had to slow down.

He looked at me in amazement. I met his gaze with a sultry stare while smacking his manhood against my face. He loved the sight of me beating it against my lips, and I could feel a torrent of my natural juices sliding down to my thighs. I took my time getting off the shower floor and turned off the water. The room was cloudy with steam and filled with the scent of sex.

"Follow me," I told him.

Michael and I dried off just enough to not make a wet mess of the bed but didn't waste time with the process.

"Why don't you lay down on your stomach," he suggested.

The bedroom was dimly lit with a breeze from a ceiling fan whirring above. Aside from the night song of crickets and other insects stirring outside, it was silent. I arched my back and positioned myself on the bed on all fours, crawling toward the headboard knowing he was watching my every move. I stopped and parted my legs to give him a deeper view.

"You are so beautiful," he admired. Michael caressed my calves, inner thighs, behind, small of my back and up my spine. He tugged at my hair, clasping a handful before releasing and bending down to kiss me again.

I started to quiver, my body impatient for him to mount me. "Give it to me," I didn't want to wait anymore. "I want to feel it now."

He punished me with extended foreplay. Michael was always a master at pacing with incredible control of his desire and stamina. He enjoyed seeing me lust for him. I wanted him relentlessly.

I flipped over on my back and sat up so I could yank him toward me. "Get over here." I pulled at his thick wrists and ordered him to the bed. "Fuck me," I demanded. "Now." The longer he made me wait, the more assertive I became. Before he could speak I took his dick into my hands and stroked it to a bulging erection. I then brought the head to my wet folds of and rubbed it to the point of my clitoris hardening against it. I rubbed us together until the heat of longing was unbearable.

"You're a waterfall. I love it," Michael rasped as he placed his entire palm over my pussy. "Feels incredible." He closed his eyes and tilted his head in pleasure as my liquidity coated his hand. "Oh, fuck!" He yelled in excitement and in one swift motion, pulled me toward the edge of the bed so my legs bent at the knees and my back and bottom lay flat on the sheets.

Michael grabbed a condom and tore the wrapper off with his teeth. Finally, it was time! Waves of lust enveloped me as I relaxed my thighs to prepare myself for his entrance. I felt my hips gyrating before he even pushed into me. The fire inside me soon raged to a blaze when Michael was ready with the protection. He pulled my legs against his chest so my feet pointed toward the ceiling. He spanked my clitoris and wet lips with his solid arousal.

"Put it in," I pleaded. The wait was unbearable, and he loved it.

When he finally slid in it was like fireworks penetrating a thunderstorm. He grunted in guttural pleasure as he entered into the comfort of my womb. He gripped me at the ankles and stroked me with years' worth of desire. I clenched the sheets as he drilled his thickness inside of me. He moved slowly at first, with careful attention to my reactions.

"That feels so good," I curled my legs around his neck and pulled him down closer to me.

I squeezed him into a snug fit and my eyes met his. He held my gaze intensely and slowed down just to dwell in me. He felt so different from my husband. A part of me did wish them to both be there in that moment. I imagined Michael holding his position while Phillip walked over from the side with his eager cock aimed at my mouth. I visualized sucking it while Michael began to stroke again. *Dear Lord.* I shocked myself with the fantasy. I didn't know if I should feel like a goddess or a slut, but I knew the thoughts propelled me into my first orgasm a lot faster than I'd hoped. I couldn't stop it if I tried. My whole body became rigid as I grinded and thrust and bucked on Michael's dick until I exploded all over it.

"Oh, yes!" Michael rode the wave of my climax and began to plow into me with speed and strength.

He placed a hand around my neck and kept pounding me. The choke shocked me at first and I wasn't sure if I liked it. But I didn't want to ruin his orgasm, and I trusted him so I let it go. The more excited he got, the more he held me down. My initial fear faded. I liked the aggression. It was different. *What was happening to me?* I tried to stay in the moment but still wondered what it meant that I liked a dangerous move like that.

"God, you feel amazing." Michael broke my thoughts.

He steadied himself on the bed, planting his fists beside me. He slowed down and changed his stroke to a grinding, circular motion without breaking our stare. He licked his lips and bit the bottom one as he focused on me even more. The energy between us was unrelenting. Ever knowing the needs of my body, he quietly pulled out to give me a chance to recover from my orgasm. Michael caressed me from head to toe and very delicately began to go down on me again. It felt so incredible that I began to melt. I opened my legs wider with each leisure flick of his tongue. He stopped here and there to look at me and smile but soon began spreading me open for his kisses me again while stroking himself with his other hand. Moments later I was ready for him to dive back in.

"Come here," I tugged him by his ears. "I'm ready for you."

Hey laid on top of me with all of his weight pressing against me on the strewn sheets.

"Fuck me," I whispered in his ear while dragging my nails across his back. "I can take it. I want it. Do it!"

Michael complied. "You like that?" He asked knowing full well what the answer was.

"Yes..." The bed rocked and I found myself breathing heavier through gritted teeth. My legs began to quake.

Sweat built on his forehead as he drilled me again. Michael angled himself so his next dips inside me were sideways. At that moment, I lost all composure. I panted with excitement as he glided in me at the perfect slant. He knew that was my favorite position. With each stroke, I felt seduced beyond measure. I ran my hands up his forearms, enjoying the feel of his veins popping from his tense physique and my mind briefly ventured back to my husband.

I want you to have the time of your life, he'd said. *Fuck him knowing I want you to have the experience.* The memories make me shudder inside. *Fuck him beyond his belief,* Phillip had said. *Give him the best of you.* As my body lay at the mercy of Michael's stellar performance, my thoughts were a maze of kinky visualizations. How would it feel to have Phillip sitting across the room watching Michael give it to me? What if he were stroking himself at the sight—or tied up with only his eyes being able to enjoy the view. How hard would he get? How long could he stand it? The illusions made me gush between my legs.

"Shit!" Michael felt the sticky water of my lust pour over him. "You feel amazing," moaned.

The more I thought of Phillip and Michael, the closer I got to another climax. The ecstasy of it all made my walls stiffen around Michael.

"Deeper," I begged, clinging to him. Our bodies became pools of sweaty flesh. "Harder!"

I couldn't hold it any longer. "Yes, yes!" I screamed in riotous pleasure as Michael's next several strokes brought me to an open-mouthed but deeply silent, earth-shattering climax. Michael made me forget how to breathe, and a vision of Phillip flashed before my eyes at the moment of release. I imagined them both naked at my side, four hands wiping my body down like attendants to a goddess. God, I'm a lucky woman. Michael finally released shortly after me and I couldn't wait for the next round.

3

"I love the way your hair falls through my fingers."

Michael's piercing eyes were the first thing I saw when I woke up hours later. "You were watching me sleep?" I was a mixture of flattered and embarrassed.

"Just a for a little while," he smiled. "I'm sorry, I couldn't help myself."

I grew bashful. "It's fine. Good morning to *you*."

"Morning, my love. So, did you enjoy last night?"

"Of course I did!"

"I'm just checking, because I know I had a great time with you."

"It was amazing. Just like I remember."

"Mm. Music to my ears! Tell me more," he begged.

I smirked, but gave in. "When your fingertips touch any part of me, it's like ... like my body catapults into a place of unbound passion. Unrivaled stimulation. I just ... I become undone, you know?"

"Oh, I know." Michael took a deep breath as if to inhale my words. "The same can be said for you. You feel so good, Leela. I could still smell you in my dreams."

Oh my. I felt a jolt between my legs but kept my composure.

"Thank you. I've barely gotten started with what I have planned for you," I teased.

"Oh really?

"Yes, really!" I refused to give him any more details in the moment.

We continued to cuddle and have pillow talk until it was time to grab a bite to eat and head out for the afternoon. Though we weren't on the island to behave like typical tourists, Michael did book a few activities for us to enjoy during the day.

"I'm looking forward to horseback riding on the beach," I told him as we ate breakfast. "I've never done it before."

"Me either, but it looks like a lot of fun. I had a feeling you'd like it." He winked.

"Great choice." I smiled and took a moment to check my phone. I could feel it vibrating in the pocket of my robe. "I'm sorry, Michael. I need to take this." It was Phillip.

"Sure." He smiled and nodded affirmatively.

I slipped into the closest bathroom to take the call. I wasn't sure why I felt like I needed so much privacy from Michael, but the move was instinctual. "Hi, baby," I answered.

"Hey, is everything going okay? I haven't heard from you much so I'm just checking in."

"I'm fine, hun. I'm sorry I didn't text you this morning. I woke up late, but everything is going well."

Phillip and I chatted a little longer before I ended the call. I could hear Michael cleaning up after I disconnected. *What am I doing?* The reality of my actions, where I was, and what was about to come fell over me like a curtain dropping from its rod. Even though I wanted this, I was still racked with conflicting feelings. Could I really go back home and sleep with Phillip without a stricken conscience? What about Michael? He seemed genuinely let down that I wasn't single and clearly thought he was going to have more of me than a weekend fling here and there.

"Leela? Everything okay?" Michael called from the kitchen.

"Everything is fine. I'll be right there!" I closed my eyes and exhaled. *Relax,* I told myself. *Just go with the flow.* It was so much easier said than done. A part of me was worried sick about Phillip, but I decided to really try to be in the moment – to experience the weekend the way I'd fantasized about it for months. This was my time. Moments later, I felt Michael's presence near the bathroom door. I stood still, waiting for him to walk by but it seemed as though he was lingering, listening. I wasn't sure. Maybe I was paranoid. I swatted my chaotic thoughts away, washed my hands and returned to the kitchen. Michael wasn't in there. In fact, the villa was still. Not even a breeze wafted through.

"Mike?"

"I'm back here, darling," he called from the bedroom.

"Where?" I still didn't see him when I followed his voice.

"Here," he emerged from the balcony off the master suite. "You want to get ready to go now?"

"Sure, sure. What were you doing out there?"

"Just taking in some fresh air. Was that your husband?"

"Huh?"

"On the phone?"

"Oh, yes!" I'd drifted away from the moment mid-conversation, still thinking of Phillip. I didn't know if what I was feeling was anxiety or remorse. And if it was the latter, was it for sleeping with Michael or not telling Michael about Phillip earlier? My emotions were a cluster-fuck. "He was just checking in on me. I'd promised I'd text him every morning to let him know I was all right."

"How thoughtful."

"Well, of course. He's my –"

"Husband. I know," Michael interrupted curtly. "Anyway, be sure to put on mosquito repellent and sun screen," his voice and face changed to a smile, "and bring a bottle of water for today, too. It's gonna be a hot one!"

"I will, thanks." *WHAT THE HELL AM I DOING?* Michael's flippant tone made me momentarily uneasy. Was he jealous?

He slid behind me and put his arms around me before I could

quiz myself more. "I can't wait to spend the day with you." His beard grazed my cheek. It felt good.

"Me too." I turned to offer my cheek for him to kiss. He didn't miss a beat, planting a seductive French kiss on my skin. "Mm. Don't start, or we won't get out of here on time for our tour. I don't want to miss it."

"We have a few minutes."

"No. We should get going or I will end up riding something other than a horse in here ... and I guarantee I will be at it for more than just a few minutes!" I teased.

Michael was amused. "That's not a bad idea! To hell with that excursion then."

"I'm getting dressed," I said, and slipped out of his grasp. I smiled at him. "We have all night for that. Let's get out of here and enjoy the day!"

"Fine, fine," he said, feigning defeat.

IT WAS a gorgeous day with a perfect breeze sweeping over the ocean. The tour Michael arranged for us was private. It was amazing to have almost an entire stretch of white-sand beach to ourselves, along with the horses and guide. A slow gallop along the shore eventually led to a trot into the glimmering waves breaking on the shore. Michael and I rode side by side atop handsome stallions in a pool of daylight. The experience was thrilling. Though it was a steamy afternoon by the middle of our ride, a youthful wind whisked over us every now and again to cut through the heat. Sweat slid down the surface of my skin and cool seawater splashed at my feet. It was truly a gorgeous day.

"Having a good time?" Michael beamed. Clearly, he was.

"I am! This is so exciting and fun. Thank you."

"My pleasure, baby." He winked and blew me a kiss.

We ended up having quite an adventure-filled day. Not long after our horseback ride on the beach, we had lunch and wandered over to another beach where Michael talked me into trying parasailing.

"You've never done it?" He was shocked at my confession to never having tried.

"Nope. It looks scary."

"Nonsense! It's peaceful. Come on. You've got to try it with me."

"I don't know." Something about being tethered to a small boat and then reeled out into the skies seemed more panic-inducing than relaxing.

"Leela," Michael took my hand. "I'll be right there with you. Trust me. You'll love it. Why don't you give it a shot?"

Against my gut feeling to continue balking, I decided to give in and try something new. "Fine. But you better be right," I pushed him playfully.

"That's my girl! You won't regret it, I promise." He led me to a pop-up tent and table where beach workers were signing people up for water sports.

I trusted Michael and coerced myself into relaxing. I knew that this was something Phillip would likely never be interested in, as he is terrified of heights. The fact that I had an alternate to my husband was an arousing thought. *What the hell*, I figured. *Let's do it!*

It didn't take long for us to be ushered on to a boat with a few other tourists and gently sailed out to sea. The farther we got from the shore the more my nerves tried to rise again but I shoved them down. When it was time for Michael and me to get strapped in and sent up in the air, I was a ball of excitement. I'd given in to the moment and enjoyed every second of our adventure at sea. The views became more breathtaking the farther we tethered away from the boat. Dazzling blue waters and warm ocean breezes blowing over us captivated me. To be able to see the shoreline from that perspective was more spectacular than I thought it would be, and with Michael next to me, made the moment all the more magical.

The experience ended too soon. I could have stayed beneath the clouds longer than the twenty minutes we were allotted for our sail. I had to give it to Michael. He was right. I loved it!

"Thanks for making me try something new," I told him once we were safely back in the boat.

"There's so much more I have in store for you – if I just get the chance."

I took his hand in mine. "You will."

He clasped my fingers tighter. "I hope so."

I rested my head on his shoulder and we rode the rest of the way back to shore in quiet appreciation of our surroundings. When we got back on land there was already a vendor with printed pictures of us in the sky. *They're quick!*

"Want to get it?" Michael asked me.

"Sure." I couldn't help myself. I loved the thought of hanging on to the memory.

Michael beamed and bought two copies. "I had such an amazing time with you!" He grabbed my hand and led the way.

We got back to the villa, and to my surprise a gorgeous dinner was set up on the beach behind the house.

"I thought you would like this," Michael said proudly. "By the time we take a shower everything will be ready for a great night."

"This is beautiful, thank you!"

"I want you to remember every detail of this trip. I want you to remember me."

"I could never forget you, Michael. No matter what, you'll always have a special place in my heart."

He closed his eyes and sighed deeply. A grin spread across his face. "That means a lot to me. Thank you."

Before I could speak again, I felt my phone vibrating. I knew it was Phillip without looking. I hesitated to pull it out to respond but did so anyway. I had to remind myself that though I wanted to have a great time with Michael that weekend, my husband came first.

"Everything okay over there?" Michael glanced over.

"Oh yeah, just texting Phillip a quick update on my trip." I thought I saw him rolling his eyes, but I could have been mistaken. *I think he* is *jealous*, the thought whisked through my mind faster than I could think to stop it. "I'm back in the moment now," I told Michael. Juggling the two of them was becoming trickier than I thought.

I slid my phone back into my bag and paid him my full attention.

My gut was starting to tell me that I should be more discreet next time. I sighed. These are the unpredictable things, feelings and moments that come up when delving into this lifestyle. Granted, I brought it on myself by hiding my marriage from Michael. I was selfish, I admit it. I just hoped the rest of the weekend went well so I could process it all on my way home and figure out what I was going to do next.

"I sure am hungry, are you?" I asked. I wanted to change the subject.

"Yes, yes, I am. Dinner should be ready soon so let's get ready to enjoy the night."

"I can't wait. The setup looks beautiful!" I meant it.

It had been years since Phillip and I had dinner on the beach. I remember it being incredibly romantic. The soundscape of the ocean, eating by torchlight and being surrounded by rose petals was a scene I could never forget. That night with Michael, a path of lights staked into the sand lead to us to a teepee-style tent with a quaint table for two set to overlook the sea. He'd changed into a tightly-fitting T-shirt and stylish jeans. His cologne smelled like heaven and the confidence and masculinity he projected made me feel like I was not with a man but a king.

"Please, have a seat," he said with a grin before pulling out my chair for me. He brushed my hair behind my ear with his fingers and looked at me as if I were the only woman on earth. He let his fingers gently caress my neck, shoulder, back and down my arm before taking his seat.

My body began to tremble. "This is so sweet," I confessed. The menu looked delicious and every other detail about the evening was tended to. "Thank you."

"It's my pleasure."

The night flew by with conversation and heavy flirtation. We'd gone through almost two bottles of wine before we retreated inside the villa for the evening. Michael said he'd need the liquid courage for plans I'd had for him.

"Are you sure you're ready to go there?" I gave him one last opportunity to back out of what was sure to be a night of consummate vulnerability for him.

"No, it was my idea. I think I can handle it and you're the only one I trust to go to that level of kink with," he grinned nervously. The king from dinner was quickly dissolving into a bashful jack ready to bow before his queen.

"All right." I was eager to bend him to my will.

In one of our many text conversations before that weekend, Michael confessed to being curious about prostate stimulation. *From what I understand, the orgasms are more powerful from it*, he'd said. I was shocked and intrigued as he told me that he wanted to try it if I were interested. I was, and it was time to bring that fantasy to life. While he freshened up in the bathroom, I dimmed the lights and quietly put a pair of handcuffs, a blindfold and a few other items inside one of the nightstands. I was just about ready by the time he emerged, but couldn't find my cell to start a playlist I'd created for us.

"Have you seen my phone?" I asked him the moment he walked in.

"No, I haven't. When's the last time you saw it?"

"I don't know – before dinner maybe? Or during? I actually can't remember."

"I don't remember seeing you with it, or seeing it laying around anywhere, but I'll keep an eye out for it."

"Thanks. I'm just going to check the kitchen and the living room."

"Do you really need it right now?" He looked disappointed.

"I had something on it I wanted you to hear."

Michael perked up. "Oh really?"

"Yes, really," I smirked. "I'll be right back!" I couldn't find my phone anywhere that I'd been in the villa that day. I double-checked my purse and several rooms in the house. I hoped I hadn't left it out by the beach. Just when I was about to tell Michael I would check there as a last resort, he surprised me.

"I found it!" He called from the bedroom.

"Where was it?"

"Between the bed and the nightstand."

That was odd ... especially for the cell to be between *his* side of the bed and the night table.

"Here you go," he offered.

I hesitated to reach for the phone, still stuck in my thoughts.

"Leela?"

"Mm?"

"Here you go, baby," he outstretched his hand to return my mobile.

I took it and opened my music streaming app to find the playlist I'd wanted to play for the night. After queuing the music, I dimmed the lights and tried to relax. I made a sincere effort to get back into the mood I'd initially been in before the phone went missing, but a little part of me felt off. While Michael got comfortable in the bed, I sent Phillip a message to tell him I loved him and that though I was having a great time, I was looking forward to coming home. It was the truth. This fantasy was a bit more fun in my head than in reality, but I had two more nights to make it as epic as I'd hoped it was going to be.

I miss you and I'm looking forward to you coming home too. Phillip wrote back. *But as long as you're having a good time, I'm good. Send a pic if you can!*

I couldn't help but respond with a devilish smiley to his request for a photo. I didn't know if I would take one – it felt invasive to Michael – but the thought was dangerously fascinating. Phillip was such a naughty man! Chatting with him put me more in the mood despite texting discretely to placate Michael's feelings. His jealousy was no longer a figment of my imagination. I knew it was real, but I also knew it was my fault, so I was doing my best to assuage him. *Selfish*, I again thought, but I was in too deep to pull out.

"Get over here woman," Michael beckoned and I stood facing him.

Before he could speak again, I pushed him back on the bed and told him to lay on his stomach. I reached for my phone once more to turn the volume of the music up before reaching for the blindfold on the nightstand and placing it over Michael's eyes. He squirmed in nervous excitement.

"Relax," I assured him as I began to kiss his shoulders, arms, back and down his spine. "Breath," I comforted him.

As the seconds slid by and we got deeper into the night, Michael's body became my playground. Between my gentle touches and deliberately slow pace, he opened up to me in a way neither of us had ever experienced. Bringing him to a forbidden place of pleasure and seeing him buck and grind, and gyrate and grip the sheets set a dark part of me ablaze. This man was mysterious. He made me feel powerful, and he sent a force of desire through my body that challenged every other sexual experience I'd ever had in my life. The access he'd given me enlivened me and a river pooled at my womb. I paused only to admire his muscular body under the dim lights: bound, blindfolded and beautifully at my mercy. As I gazed at him, I remembered Phillip's request for a photo. I was tempted to take one but felt terrible about violating Michael's trust. Milliseconds felt like an eternity as I decided what I was going to do. Phillip was my husband, and I owed him something for allowing this, I rationalized. Plus, I wanted to remember the experience long after the weekend passed. I exhaled, reached for my phone and snapped a photo under the guise of replaying a song.

I caressed Michael's body while I moved the picture to a secure folder on my phone. I didn't want to take any chances of him seeing it. One part of me felt a thrill; another felt ashamed. I blocked out all of my emotions and redirected my full attention to Michael. I soon set him free and the night went on with catapulting moments of pleasure mixed with tender moments of simple embracing. We fell asleep in each other's arms on twisted sheets under glowing lights.

4

The morning after, I woke up alone and uncertain. The villa was still. I didn't see or hear Michael while I searched the bed for my bra and panties. I called out to him but was greeted with only silence. How could this man move about so quietly all the time? I reached for my phone to check for any messages from Phillip – there was one from the night before wishing me a good time and hoping for an image. Without thinking about it, I exported the photo I'd taken and sent it to him.

"Good morning, gorgeous," Michael scared the life out of me. He walked into the room like a drafty breeze.

"Good morning." I gulped, unready for his presence. "How are you?"

"I'm fine, darling, and you? Did you sleep well?"

"Good. I slept deeply."

He took a seat on the bed and looked me directly in the eyes for more than a few seconds before speaking again. "I don't want you to go home." Michael spoke without expression.

"What?" I couldn't tell if he was serious or not.

"I don't want you to go back to your husband."

"Michael..."

He stood up and began to pace. "You could be so much happier with me."

"But I can't ... that's not what this is."

"What is it then?"

"A good time. A fun weekend. A fantasy come true."

"For you." He looked away from me when he spoke, first with his hands squarely on his hips and then tapping them at his sides.

I took a deep breath. "I know I wasn't upfront about everything, but we both knew this weekend was for a carefree time – no strings attached, but that we could keep in touch and flirt after – nothing more."

Michael spun around in a with a look in his eyes that made my heart freeze. I heard him say, "You're not leaving!" and quickly felt myself getting sucked into a vortex of his fury. This couldn't be happening!

Michael pounded the wall with his fists. "Look what you made me do!" He sneered at me.

My mind exploded. I felt like I'd been snatched into a storm and the room started to swirl. "Michael, please!" I panicked and scrambled to my feet. I'd dismissed his previous foibles too quickly and hadn't anticipated a hard switch in his personality. The sour taste of regret started draining the life from my mouth and my heartbeat began to race to a pace nearing explosion.

Michael breathed heavily and stared at me without blinking.

"Okay, calm down. Just relax a little." I had to diffuse the situation and get out of there quickly. Michael was unpredictable and I didn't want to wait around to find out what would happen next.

"Relax. Really?" He spoke with a disturbing vibration.

I couldn't find my cell, and none of my real clothes were laying around. I hurried into the closet to get what I'd hung up but the moment I stepped in was the moment my world collapsed. Michael followed me and the next thing I knew his massive arms were holding me in place and a pin prick pinched my skin. He cradled me for a few moments before spinning me free and walking out. Michael slammed the door behind him and barricaded me in.

"I don't want you to go," he spoke firmly from the other side.

"Let me out of here!" I tried to open the door forcibly, but it wouldn't budge. Anxiety and fear shuttered my mind black. I hyperventilated. I couldn't believe what was happening! "Michael, open this door! Open the door!" I pounded my fists against the wood frame until my hands felt like they were going to split open. I felt dizzy. My vision blurred and an unsteady feeling rattled my equilibrium. I slunk to the floor with a cloudy haze polluting my thoughts. I vaguely remembered the pinch to my skin as I rolled over hangers on my way down. Was I drugged?

"All you had to do was say yes, Leela. That's all you had to do. I could have protected you!" I couldn't tell if Michael's voice was a dream or reality. My consciousness wasn't concrete. I thought I heard an echo. Not long after was I out completely. I later woke up with my hands and feet bound. A cloth gagged my mouth and Michael was stroking my hair while holding my phone.

"How does it feel to be tied up and vulnerable? Do you like it?"

My head was pounding, and I felt woozy. My arm felt sore. I blinked hard to bring myself to the current moment.

"You know, while you were knocked out. I took a few photos of you. Sort of like the ones you took of me."

I jolted present. My eyes swelled with panic.

"Oh yes, I saw your text to your husband." Michael mushed my head violently. "I trusted you!"

Tears began to stream down my cheeks. "I'm sorry," I mumbled through the gag. "I'm so sorry!" I tried to move but nearly fell over. Still only wearing my bra and panties, I was Michael's captive.

"I sent your husband a message to let him know you were having a great time – that you decided to stay another day or so." Michael smiled, picked me up and laid me down on the bed on my side. He put me in a fetal position and laid down behind me.

I trembled with fear. Nothing I'd ever done or thought of in my life had prepared me for that moment. A petrified sob curdled from my throat. The more nervous I became, the closer Michael got. He placed my phone down in front of us – but out of my reach – and laid behind me in a spoon position.

"Why don't you want to stay with me?" He inched closer and put his arm around me. Michael grabbed my cell and put the camera on selfie mode.

I nearly fainted as he took a burst of shots. Would he text them to Phillip? The thought haunted me beyond belief. How did a weekend that started to nice disintegrate so rapidly?

Michael didn't say much else, he just held me, sniffing my hair and caressing my skin while planting slow kisses on my shoulder. With each connection of his lips and fingers, I felt as if I were getting singed by lightning. The feel of his breath in my ear made me cringe. Every fiber of my being was on edge, and I began silently pray to gods in whom I'd never truly believed. At that point, I'd do anything to be free!

"Do you think you'll change your mind now?" He turned me to face him and smiled. "Oh, it must be hard to talk with this in your mouth. Silly me!" Michael tugged the gag away. "There. Feel better?"

I tried to speak, but the words wouldn't come out. My heart still raced, and my hands and feet ached from being bound. Sweat and tears burned my eyes.

"Now is the perfect time to speak, Leela. Talk!" He became angry again. "This can all be very simple and painless."

The word pain dripping from his venomous lips made something inside me click. The fear that had been swallowing me began morphing into a defensive anger. I don't know how much time had gone by since I'd been his captive, but at that moment I'd decided that it was more than enough. It didn't matter if I was wrong in leading him on or not, there was no way in hell I was going to allow myself to be Michael's prisoner.

"Every time I find someone they either cheat on me or desert me. I thought you were different." Michael got up and began to pace. "I thought you were better than that, but oh, no. You're worse! You lied to me, and you betrayed me," He placed his hands on his hips and began to mumble. He drifted into his own world as if I was no longer there.

I took those free moments to sweep the room for a way to escape. There were only two ways out: the bedroom door and the balcony. There were lamps on both nightstands, and a pair of my heels weren't too far from the bed. My phone was within reach, but my hands and feet were restrained by duct tape, so it was impossible to inch toward it without Michael noticing. A flat sheet was loosely strewn about the bed and my purse was hanging on a hook on the bedroom door. There was also a hardcover book in one of the nightstands, I'd remembered. My mind raced, remembering a situational awareness class I'd once taken. Every detail mattered.

"Okay, Michael," I finally spoke to get his attention.

He spun around as if I'd snatched him from his alternate reality.

I feigned more regretful tears and spoke in a measured, defeated voice. "Maybe you're right. Maybe I would be better off with you."

His eyes sparkled in delight.

"I was wrong for what I did to you."

"You're damned right!"

"But I want to make it up to you." I took a deep breath, my heart thudding in my chest. "You're a good man. You know, this is all my fault, and I'm so sorry." I wiggled and squirmed to make my discomfort more noticeable. "Can you sit me up, please?"

He glared at me, unsure.

"Please. I just need to be in another position. And I really need to use the bathroom. But I want to talk things over with you, if you'll give me a chance to make this right."

Michael bit his bottom lip, looking as though he took the bait. He walked over and repositioned me.

"Can you help me to the bathroom?"

He released an annoyed sigh but agreed. "Fine. But don't you dare try anything!"

"Michael, I just want to pee. You can even leave the door cracked if you want. Where am I going to go anyway?"

He carried me to the bathroom.

"My panties," I said sheepishly. "I can't pull them down by myself."

Michael seemed to experience a moment of perverse joy at my dependence on him. He slid my undergarment off and helped me sit on the toilet.

"Can I have some privacy, please?"

He grunted and walked out, forgetting to leave the door cracked. Not more than ten seconds after Michael stepped out, I struggled to my feet and broke free from the duct tape around my wrists. I'd remembered seeing the move on a self-defense video. My first attempt was weak, but the second time the tape popped free. Adrenaline fueled me. I knew I didn't have much time and hurried to try and release my legs. This time the technique wasn't as clear in my head, but I found small scissors in a drawer after a quick search and cut myself free. Sweat bubbled on my forehead and streamed down my stomach and back as I maneuvered.

Michael was coming back. I felt his presence. *Shit.* I grabbed a washcloth and ran it under hot water. The moment he opened the door I swatted him across the face with the rag and tried to barrel past him into the bedroom.

"You bitch!" He grabbed me before I could escape but lost his balance and stumbled against the toilet.

I seized a can of hairspray from the counter and laced his face with it. While Michael was stunned, I snatched a removable mirror and cracked it against his head.

"Goddamn it!" He cried out, falling to the floor. Michael kicked me brutally while trying to get up.

A surge of pain bolted through my leg. I bit my lip and stifled the scream that wanted to escape from my throat. I wouldn't give Michael the satisfaction of seeing me in a weak state any longer. "Fuck you!" I grabbed that same pair of scissors that I used to free myself and slashed him across his face.

Desperation to escape turned me into a woman I didn't know I could be. Blood ran down his bald head and he laid there stunned, maimed and in disbelief. Michael had an expression on his face that looked as though I were in the wrong.

"Why would you do this to me?" he bellowed.

I knew this moment wouldn't last much longer, as he was quickly moving past processing the turn of events to a look of pure hatred. With nothing left to grab or throw and only seconds to spare, I lifted my leg and hammered my heel into his ankle with all of my strength. A bone cracked.

"You motherfucking bitch! I'm going to kill you!" he raged.

I ran into the bedroom and grabbed anything to put on. As I put one of my feet into a pants leg, I heard Michael struggling in the bathroom. I hurried to get dressed and bolted toward the bedroom door. Before I could reach it, I felt Michael's grip on the tail of my barely-buttoned blouse. I didn't look back, determined to get out.

"Get back here!" he demanded.

I clutched the doorknob only to realize that it was locked. The chaos of the moment made my mind go blank. It was a typical bedroom door lock that I could just turn to disable, but I was so panicked that just enough time passed for Michael to reach me.

I turned around ready to slash him with the scissors again, just in time to see his fist coming at me. His clumsily placed punch landed on the edge of my jaw, but it hurt like nothing I'd ever felt before. Pain and anger rose up in me, and my mind went black. I lost track of time. I forgot where I was. I acted without thought.

"Leela!" The gurgling sound of his voice brought me back.

When my vision and mind cleared, I saw Michael laying at my feet with multiple stab wounds to his face and chest. My heart stopped. I felt my fingers trembling. What just happened? Michael stopped moving but was bleeding. I looked over at my right hand and saw the bloody scissors. *Oh my God.*

As the reality of my unconscious rage became clear, fear and anxiety flooded me. Did he just die? It didn't look like he was moving. *Get out of here.* The thought boomed in my head like thunder. I ran to the bed to grab my phone and jetted out of the room. I had no idea where the car keys were or where I was going, but I had to get far away from that house.

I was a barefoot, bloodied mess running into the pristine streets of a paradise island.

"Get away, get away, get away!" I mumbled this mantra without effort until I reached the end of the block. I was heaving for air and my feet burned from running on the hot asphalt. Tears cascaded from my eyes as I struggled to dial 911. "Hello, police!" I nearly collapsed when an operator answered the phone.

I could barely speak and my body crinkled to the sidewalk as I cried my story into the phone.

"We will send someone right away," the dispatcher said. "Just try to stay calm, please ma'am," she pleaded in her foreign accent.

I sobbed. I shook. My mind felt under ambush. Everything from the night before fired throughout my head. "Do you know how soon they will –"

Just as I tried to ask another question my phone died. I was so on edge I hadn't noticed the battery running low. I wanted to wail. I desperately wanted to call Phillip, but had no way to now. My chest tightened, and it felt as though I was suffocating.

A police siren soon wailed in the distance. By this time, strangers had approached me to ask what happened. I was sure I looked like a madwoman. I could barely string together another sentence, but when I saw the cop car round the corner I suddenly felt a release of pressure from my head and lungs. Finally, help was there.

5

_____

There was such a commotion on the road. As my world closed in on me, I began noticing every detail again. Police, an ambulance, curious construction workers and nervous vacationers all buzzed about. Michael was alive. It turned out that he was only unconscious when I ran out of the villa. Perhaps all of my jabs to rend his skin with the small scissors only created shallow wounds. I don't know, but considering the fact that I was in a foreign country I was grateful that I hadn't killed him ... even though a small part of me wishes I had. Michael terrorized me in a way I could have never imagined. How could a weekend that was supposed to be filled with so much bliss turn into a whirlwind of terror?

I was overwhelmed with the attention and questioning from first responders and felt myself disconnecting from reality in the hysteria of it all.

"Leela!" A familiar voice made my heart freeze.

"Phillip?" My eyes widened to search the group of people beyond the officers in front of me. "Phillip!" It was his voice, I knew it. I couldn't have been hallucinating that.

"Oh my God, Leela," he appeared moments later from amid the crowd.

I nearly jumped with eagerness to be in his arms.

"Sir!" An officer pushed Phillip back by the chest. "Please back up."

"He's my husband," I interjected. Shame torpedoed me. "Please," I pleaded. My heart had never felt so relieved than when I saw Phillip at that moment.

The officers eyed him for a bit longer before relaxed their restriction. I collapsed in his arms. Sobs erupted from the depths of my soul.

"What happened?" Phillip held me for dear life.

"We have a few more questions before you go to the hospital to be checked out," an officer interrupted.

I didn't want to go to the hospital but refocused my attention so I could answer his questions. Phillip, only hearing the abridged tail end of what happened, listened with a sunken expression plastered on his face. I could only imagine him trying to process the sight of me, the police, the crowd and hearing what I was telling them. I could see his jaw trembling and pain mounting in his eyes.

"You should see a doctor, Leela," Phillip agreed with the officers. "I want to get you checked out and then get you out of here."

"I can see my doctor at home," I protested, but the moment the words fell from my lips I realized I'd rather not explain this situation to anyone but Phillip.

"The sooner the better to make sure whatever you were drugged with won't have any lasting effect," he insisted.

"Fine." I relented.

I was so utterly hurt, shocked, embarrassed and remorseful about everything that my physical examination became a blur. I was okay, that's all I needed to know and remember. I ached for Phillip and I to be alone. I had so many questions. What was he doing there? When did he arrive? How did he find me? What was he thinking? It would be a few hours before we were alone in a hotel room, awaiting the first flight out of the country the following morning.

"Something didn't feel right," he told me. "I got this message from your number about wanting to stay longer, but it didn't feel like you. And then when I tried calling you, I didn't get an answer."

I tried to question him more but could only cry instead.

"Call it intuition or whatever, but I just knew deep down that something was off," Phillip continued. "I checked your location and saw where you were and how long you'd been there. I had two choices: sit around waiting despite my gut feeling, or get down here and see for myself. The worst that could happen was you were safe but uncomfortable about my arrival. The alternative..." he looked at me and shook in disbelief. "Let's just say I'm happy you remembered everything about self-defense that you learned. I would have been too late to stop anything from the looks of it."

"I'm so sorry, Phillip. This is all my fault." I felt a ball lodge itself in my throat. "I had no idea things would turn out like this."

"Shh. Shh," he comforted me. "There's no sense in blaming yourself. All that matters is that you're safe now – and I'm not letting you out of my sight. I love you so much."

"I love you too!" I buried my face in the enclave of his neck and breathed in Phillip's reassuring presence. I was exhausted to the core.

WHAT HAPPENED with Michael that weekend was a life and death reminder of the problem with living for pleasure. It's addictive, and never enough. Sometimes what you have truly is enough and just because you *can* have more of what pleases you, doesn't mean that you *should*. I was only Michael's captive for a few hours, and years later the experience still haunts me.

I know that I was partly to blame. Perhaps Michael wouldn't have snapped if I'd just been honest with him about my marital status, but I was greedy. I wanted what I wanted and didn't think about his feelings. I never considered his mental state as I strung him along. There's no excuse for holding another human being against her will, but I'd be a hypocritical fool if I didn't at least admit that I shared some of the blame for putting myself in danger.

When Phillip and I first discussed opening up our marriage, we made rules. We had boundaries and an outline of what was acceptable and what wasn't. Honesty was paramount with all parties. I always told Phillip the truth about everything because at the end of the day, I was married to *him* and my allegiance was never a matter of question. Phillip trusted my judgement and never meddled much in my conversations with Michael. He didn't know that Michael was unaware of my marital status and that hurt him.

"How could you leave out such an important detail? Leela, I would have never agreed to this with that as a wild card!"

"I'm sorry!"

Days and weeks after the incident, Phillip and I would get into heated talks about what happened; but in the end, we reconciled and decided to retreat into each other rather than fall apart. I loved him more than anything in this world and recommitted my love to him. My pursuit of pleasure had taken me to the edge of bliss and nearly into death. It was the most extreme circumstance that I could have ever been in ... and a reality check to the dangers of dishonesty and greed. Thankfully, I made it out alive with a husband who still honored his pledge to love me – for better or worse.

www.ingramcontent.com/pod-product-compliance
Lightning Source LLC
Chambersburg PA
CBHW050908120626
46554CB00003B/1080